Disney · PIXAR

Cars
TOON

MATER THE GREATER

★ ★ ★ AND MORE TALL TALES! ★ ★ ★

 publications international, ltd.

When Mater visits Tokyo, everyone crowds around to watch him compete in a drift race. Look for these cars who can't wait for the race to start!

¡Olé! In Spain, El Materdor bravely battles bulldozers. Search the stands for these red items that might distract the dozers.

This sign

This gas can

This beret

This poster

This Spanish/English dictionary

This map of Spain

Look! It's the famous daredevil, Mater the Greater! Search the stadium for these props he needs to perform his death-defying stunts.

These cones

This cannon

This helmet

This ramp

This flaming hoop

This rocket pack

This target

Oh, no! There's a fire at the old gasoline and match factory! Mater to the rescue! As Mater fights the blaze, look for these things that could fuel the fire.

Lamp oil

Fireworks

Gas can

Stack of newspapers

Old rags

Crate of matches

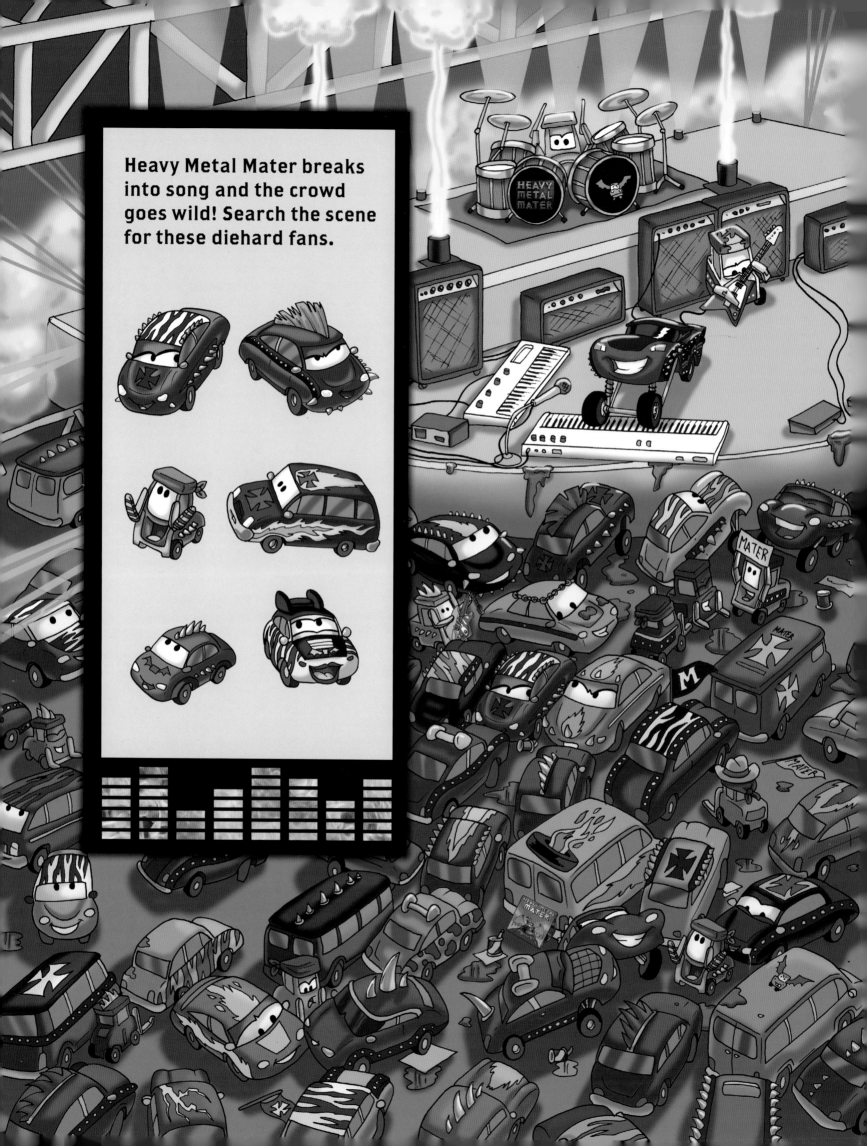

Heavy Metal Mater breaks into song and the crowd goes wild! Search the scene for these diehard fans.

In the wrestling ring, Mater and Lightning McQueen transform into The Tormentor and Frightening McMean! Hunt for these cars in the crowd who will watch them face off against Dr. Frankenwagon and The Monster.

I-Screamer

Mia & Tia

Paddy O'Concrete

The Super Fan

Rastacarian

Dr. Feel Bad

When Mater tries to free the UFO from Parking Area 51, he gets some help from the Mother Ship just in the nick of time! Look for these scientists and military personnel who were hot on their heels.

In Tokyo, Lightning saved Mater from a ninja attack! Mater will have to steer clear of even more trouble to make it to the top of Tokyo Tower. Find these ninjas that are hiding nearby.

Race back to Tokyo to find these colorful elements on the glowing signs.

El Materdor's fans shower him with flowers. Run back to the bullring to find two dozen red roses.

"Two buckteeth for one buck!" Vendors in the stands sell fake buckteeth to Mater the Greater's biggest fans. Return to the stadium to find these fans that are wearing fake teeth.

Soon Rescue Squad Mater will need to refill his water tank. Help him find the hose that's hooked up to the fire hydrant.

Head back to Heavy Metal Mater's concert to find these souvenirs that his fans will take home.

Return to the wrestling ring to find 10 fans who got The Tormentor's autograph.

Mater once mistook a flying hubcap for a UFO. Go back to the desert to find these other things that look a little like flying saucers.

When Mater wins the drift race, he will be declared the King of All Drifters! Slide back to the Tokyo race scene to find these oil barrels he will have to dodge along the way.

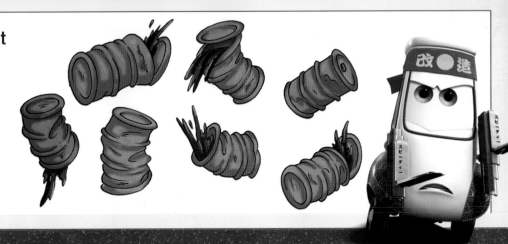

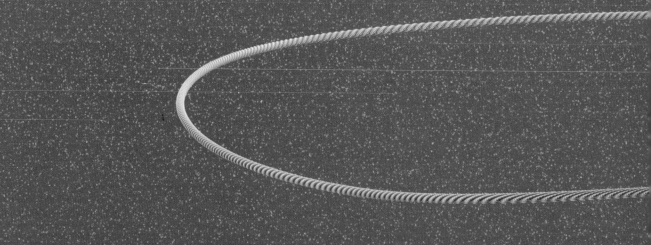
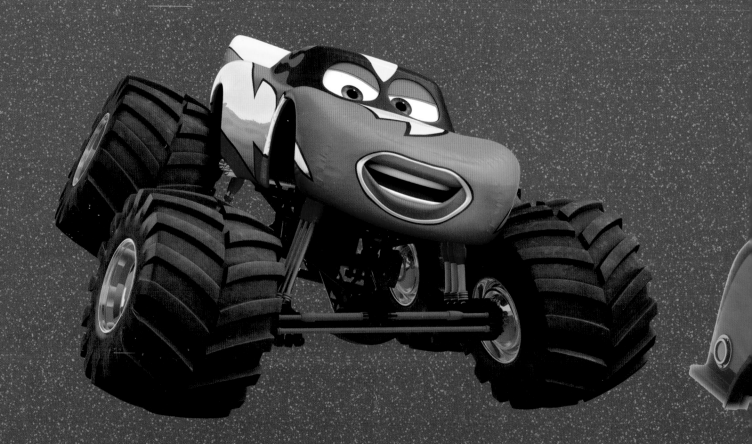